The Twelve UNICORNS of Christmas

Timothy Knapman

Ada Grey

EGMONT

On the **first day** of Christmas,
my parents gave to me . . .

1 sparkling Christmas tree!

To Margie, who loves
Christmas and unicorns, with love – T.K.

For Babs and Becky – A.G.

EGMONT
We bring stories to life

First published in Great Britain 2019 by Egmont UK Limited

The Yellow Building, 1 Nicholas Road, London W11 4AN

www.egmont.co.uk

Text copyright © Timothy Knapman 2019

Illustrations copyright © Ada Grey 2019

The author and illustrator have asserted their moral rights.

ISBN 978 1 4052 9527 7

A CIP catalogue record for this title is available from the British Library.

And a real-life UNICORN!

On the **second day** of Christmas,
my unicorn gave to me . . .

2 festive jumpers!

But my unicorn was much better at
being sparkly than he was at knitting!

On the **third day** of Christmas,
my parents gave to us . . .

3 empty stockings!

On the **fourth day** of Christmas:

ding-dong!

There was someone at the door . . .

4 Grandmas and Grandpas!

Grandma loved meeting my unicorn.

On the **fifth day** of Christmas,
my grandma gave to me . . .

5 twinkly unicorn lights!

I hoped Santa would see them
and find his way to our house
on Christmas Eve.

On the **sixth day** of Christmas,
my parents gave to us . . .

6 scrummy mince pies!

My unicorn loved mince pies . . .

Uh-oh,
perhaps a bit too much!

On the **seventh day** of Christmas,
my unicorn gave to me . . .

7 clockwork Santas!

So we had a big race.

Ready,

steady,

GO!

On the **eighth day** of Christmas,
my parents made with me . . .

8 snow unicorns!

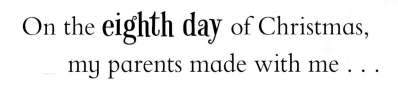

My snow unicorn was the best . . .

. . . until it fell over!

On the **ninth day** of Christmas, my friends all got from me . . .

9 cards with unicorns on them!

I was being very neat,

but my unicorn loved to scribble

and make lots of mess.

On the **tenth day** of Christmas,
my unicorn gave to me . . .

10 cake decorations!

Achoo!

WOW – unicorn sneezes are made of glitter!

On the **eleventh day** of Christmas,
there were some people at the door . . .

11 carol singers!

My unicorn loved singing,
but he wasn't very good at it!

On the night before Christmas,
my unicorn looked a little bit less sparkly . . .

So that night I wished that Santa would bring my unicorn a present to make him feel better.

And when we woke on
Christmas morning,
we heard a funny noise . . .

So we went downstairs and you'll **never guess** what we saw . . .

On the **twelfth day** of Christmas, Santa
brought 11 new friends so suddenly there were . . .

12 UNICORNS!

Merry Christmas!